Some Kind of Hero

by Lesley Choyce

The man driving the ambulance fired up the siren and we sped off across the soccer field and past the high school. Alan was unconscious. His skin looked something awful. The ambulance lady in the back had put an oxygen mask over his face. As we went out the driveway, I looked back at the brick school building through the back window. I had a feeling that things there would never be quite the same after this.

Y0-BDZ-132

Other books by Lesley Choyce

Novels:

Downwind
Magnificent Obsessions
Skateboard Shakedown
The Hungry Lizards
The Second Season of Jonas MacPherson
Wave Watch
Wrong Time, Wrong Place

Short story collections:

Billy Botzweiler's Last Dance
Coming Up for Air
Conventional Emotions
Eastern Sure
The Dream Auditor

Non-fiction:

An Avalanche of Ocean
December Six/The Halifax Solution

Poetry:

Fast Living
Re-inventing the Wheel
The End of Ice
The Man Who Borrowed the Bay of Fundy
The Top of the Heart

series

2000

LESLEY CHOYCE

Some Kind of Hero

Maxwell Macmillan Canada

Copyright © 1991 by Maxwell Macmillan Canada Inc.
All rights reserved. No part of this book may be
reproduced or transmitted in any form or by any means,
electronic or mechanical, including photocopying,
recording, or by any information storage and retrieval
system, without permission in writing from the publisher.

Maxwell Macmillan Canada
1200 Eglinton Ave. E., Suite 200
Don Mills, Ontario M3C 3N1

ISBN 0-02-954082-8

GENERAL EDITOR: Paul Kropp
SERIES EDITOR: Sandra Gulland
TITLE EDITOR: Fran Murphy
DESIGNER: Brant Cowie
ILLUSTRATOR: Julie de Bellefeuille
COVER PHOTOGRAPHY: Peter Paterson

1 2 3 4 5 6 95 94 93 92 91
Printed and bound in Canada

CANADIAN CATALOGUING IN PUBLICATION DATA
Choyce, Lesley, 1951-
    Some kind of hero

(Series 2000)
ISBN 0-02-954082-8

I. Title. II. Series.
PS8555.H668S6 1991   jC813'.54   C91-094459-8
PZ7.C46So 1991

To Nicole Meaney,
of Sidney Mines, Nova Scotia.

CONTENTS

CHAPTER 1

It was the first big game of the year and nothing could have kept me away. Queen Elizabeth High was playing Halifax West in what was going to be one very serious game of soccer. When Alan spotted me, he ran over and gave me a big hug. "I'm glad you're here, Tina. You always bring me good luck," he said.

The rest of the team was headed our way. Rick looked at me, then at Alan. He swerved and smashed right into Alan, knocking him off balance. "Sorry, man," he said. "Guess I wasn't watching where I was going."

Alan looked puzzled, but I knew what it was all about. Rick was still pretty ticked off that I had dumped him, even though it happened three months ago.

Alan just shrugged. He gave me that cute, goofy smile of his and ran to join the other

guys at the bench. Coach Kenner began to read off the names of those who would play first string. As he called them off one by one, they ran onto the field. Then the coach stopped. He scratched his head and couldn't make up his mind about something. There was only one more slot to be filled. He looked at Rick, then at Alan. Finally he pointed a finger at Alan. "Go," he said.

Alan raced onto the field. Rick yelled something at the coach, but Kenner ignored him.

I looked around to see if Alan's mom was at the game. Fortunately, she was nowhere in sight. Alan's mother thought I was bad news. Maybe she thought I was into drugs or something. Alan figured it was just the way I looked—my long black hair and my shredded pants. Maybe it was because I did all my shopping at the Salvation Army that she didn't think I was good enough for him.

Of course, Alan didn't care what she thought about me. That was just one of the things I liked about him.

The only person who ever got to Alan was Rick. Rick had a way of putting people down, especially guys who were friends of old girlfriends. He couldn't handle the idea that I'd dumped him. In the halls he'd call me "Tina Toy" like I was some kind of stupid doll.

I could just ignore Rick, but Alan couldn't. They both played halfback on the Q.E.H. soccer team. They were both fast and they both had legs like lightning when it came to kicking soccer balls into the net. But every time Alan made the smallest mistake at practice, Rick was all over him. He'd say, "What's the matter, Al, legs turn to mush again?" Or, "C'mon dude, you can't wimp out like that. Your girlfriend, Tina Toy, is watching." And Rick's theme song on the field, the phrase he said over and over to Alan was, "You'll never do anything great unless you take a few chances. You just always want to play it safe. Safe is for suckers."

The whistle blew. The game began and players were charging all over the field like angry animals. Rick was going nuts on the sidelines. I watched as he yelled something at Coach Kenner again, but the coach told him to shut up.

Halifax West had the ball. They were only metres from our goal when I saw Alan try to slip himself between two of their players like a quarter being dropped into a pay phone. He ducked low, got control of the ball and shot out down the field. He made a pass to Wicket out on end. As soon as Wicket was surrounded by Halifax West defencemen, the ball was shot back to Alan.

I held my breath as he set himself up to make the kick. The ball was off. A fullback tried to kick the ball as it shot free from Alan, but he missed and his foot came up hard, catching Alan right under the ribs. You could hear this awful thud. I grabbed my own sides and could feel the pain as Alan fell to the ground.

The heavy fullback fell right on top of him. I heard a terrifying scream come out of Alan. That's when I knew he was in trouble. Alan was not a screamer. I'd never heard him give the slightest whimper from any pain, ever. He is as tough as they come.

A whistle blew. The ball had missed the net. Nobody knew what I knew. I hopped over the rickety snow fence and ran onto the field. The referee pulled the goon off of Alan, but Alan was still curled up on the grass.

Coach Kenner yelled at me to get off the field. He probably thought, *a kid falls down in a game, big deal*. But I knew better.

The ref had his hand on Alan's shoulder and the other players had moved back. Alan was gulping for air and let out a terrible sort of moan, like he was trying to cry, but couldn't. I could see his skin was clammy and pale. I tried to hear what he was saying and finally made out the words, "Help me."

Coach Kenner was still acting like it was nothing. Rick came over, ranting and raving. He was playing it for all it was worth. "Look at this guy. He gets the wind knocked out of him and he wimps out. What a joke."

I gave Rick a look that would have made any creature with even half a brain run for cover. "Call an ambulance," I told the coach, my voice shaking.

Now the ref was bending over Alan. He looked up at Coach Kenner. "She's right," he said. "Better get one here quick."

CHAPTER 2

The coach asked if anyone from the team would volunteer to go with Alan to the hospital.

"I'm going," I said. I wanted to be with Alan and I wasn't going to let anyone stop me. Coach Kenner looked at me like he wasn't going to let me go. Then he saw that I was dead serious and he just nodded.

There was a woman who came with the ambulance, a black lady who took control of the situation. "Get in honey," she said to me. "Just sit tight and let us do our work."

I got in. The man driving the ambulance fired up the siren and we sped off across the soccer field and past the high school. Alan was unconscious. His skin looked something awful. The ambulance lady in the back had put an oxygen mask over his face. As we went out the driveway, I looked back at the brick school building through the back window. I had a feeling that things there would never be quite the same after this.

As we drove on, the woman studied Alan's breathing. She looked up at me and tried to fake a smile. "What's your name?" she asked me.

"Tina."

"I'm Martha. You know this guy?"

Right then I tried to talk, but couldn't. Nothing came out. I was that scared. Martha seemed to understand what Alan meant to me.

"Hang onto that strap," she said, pointing to a rope loop above my head. I grabbed it. Then she yelled to the driver, "I think this calls for a little more action, Vince."

Vince hit the siren again and punched the gas pedal to the floor. We flew around a corner and I held on to the strap. Martha smiled at me again—a warm smile. "Vince likes it when he gets to drive fast," she said, pretending to me that it was all a game. Maybe she wanted me to think that Alan wasn't as bad off as I knew he was.

"Alan?" I said, leaning over him.

There was no response. Martha pulled me away to sit down. "He's unconscious," she said. "He can't answer you right now."

At the hospital, I was pushed out of the way by two orderlies who helped wheel the stretcher into Emergency. I wanted to ask, What is it? What's wrong? Will he be O.K.? But I had given up. Nobody was about to answer my questions because nobody knew.

They wheeled Alan down a long hallway. I tried to get a good view of which room they took him into.

I sat down and tried to relax, but couldn't. Martha came in and found me sitting on the edge of the chair. "Wish I could hang around and keep you company, Tina, but I got another call." She flipped a loonie my way. "Go get a Coke," she said. "Things usually aren't as bad as they seem, believe me." She gave my hand a squeeze and then turned to go.

I was in a kind of a funny haze and I almost thought I was going to pass out, but I took a deep breath and stumbled off, looking for the pop machine. I couldn't believe this had happened. Things had been going so right for me lately. I was doing better in school. I had learned how to ignore my parents' battles. Alan was really helping me turn my life around. And now this.

I popped the loonie into the machine, but could only stand there looking at the choices. I couldn't think straight. I needed to see Alan right then. I had to make sure he was alive.

I ran down the long hallway. An orderly grabbed me and said, "You can't go down there," but I pulled away. I kept going until I saw a sign over a door that said, "EMERGENCY O.R."

Inside, I saw a little kid who was crying as he got stitches put into his cut finger. An old flabby guy without a shirt on was taking a deep breath as a doctor held a stethoscope up to his chest. Then I saw Alan, stretched out, still unconscious. Two doctors and a nurse were clustered around him. They looked very serious.

The nurse was inserting a tube into Alan's arm as I came near.

"Is he going to be all right?" I asked her.

"You shouldn't be in here," she said.

"Is he going to be all right?" I demanded.

One of the doctors, a young guy with glasses, turned to me. He was acting like this was no big deal, like it happened all the time. In a cool, clinical voice, he asked me, "Could you describe the accident? Please."

I told him what had happened and he nodded. He turned to the other doctor. "Almost certainly the liver. Internal bleeding. Let's get him stabilized and run some tests."

"What's his name?" the doctor asked me, again sounding like this was all matter-of-fact.

"Alan," I said. "Alan Richards."

The doctor bent over his patient and shined a tiny light in his eyes. "Alan, can you hear me?"

"No response," said the other doctor. "Let's get him upstairs."

The door opened and the nurse from up front came in with Alan's parents. They saw Alan stretched out unconscious on the table. His mother picked up his hand and seemed shocked by the feel of it. It was cold and clammy, I knew. I had held onto him during most of the ambulance ride and it was scary.

"We have to get him upstairs. We think there's damage to the liver. Will you go out front and fill out the permission form?"

Alan's mother started to speak to the doctors in a shaky voice. "We want a second opinion," she demanded.

"No," I blurted out. "He needs help now." I knew that minutes counted.

The doctor looked at Alan's mother, then at his father. "We can't proceed without your permission."

Mr. Richards looked at me, then at his wife. He seemed very confused. And I think he was really afraid. "Go ahead," he said to the doctor. "Please help our son." He put an arm around his wife, who nodded her head in agreement.

The doctor began to wheel Alan out of the room. As Alan's mother let go of his hand, she looked up at me. "What are you doing here?" she asked. The expression on her face burned a hole right through me.

I tried to say something, but my voice still wasn't working right. Ignoring Mrs. Richards, I tried to follow Alan to the elevator. An orderly pulled me toward a small waiting room, saying, "Calm down. Everybody here knows what they're doing. Just let them do it."

I tried to ignore him and walk in the direction they had taken Alan, but the orderly stopped me again. "You can't go down there," he said.

"Let me go," I insisted.

"Sorry, I can't."

I pulled myself free and ran for the front door. Outside, I kept on running until I was six blocks away. By then, my eyes were so filled up with tears that I couldn't see enough to keep going.

CHAPTER 3

I phoned the hospital as soon as I got home. They told me Alan was in surgery, but that I could call back around eight o'clock. After a long, nerve-racking wait, I phoned again.

"Your name please?" the lady asked.

"Tina Wright."

"You're not part of the immediate family?"

I didn't get it. Why was she putting me off? "I'm his girlfriend, O.K.?" I snapped.

"Sorry, I can't help you. Only the immediate family can talk to the doctor in charge of that case," she said. And the line went dead.

I opened my bedroom door and was ready to go back to the hospital. But my folks were downstairs. There was no way I could get out of the house without going past them.

I knew they wouldn't let me go out. I quietly slid back into my bedroom and waited for them to go to bed.

It drove me crazy, not knowing if Alan was going to be O.K. I kept thinking about all the good times we'd had together and couldn't believe all that could change so fast. Alan was the only guy I had ever known who treated me like I really mattered. Plenty of other guys had been interested in me, but always for the wrong reasons. Alan was different. In fact, I couldn't quite figure him out. Around other guys, he was just like them. I'd seen him get into fights over nothing. I'd seen him act really crude to teachers and even to the coach. But as soon as he was alone with me, he had this other side to him. He was kind and gentle. He really cared about how I felt.

I kept thinking back to the time my parents had been fighting and I got so upset I couldn't think straight at school. It seemed like everybody in town knew about the loud screeching battles my mom and dad were having. It made it pretty hard to go to school with everyone knowing all about it. But Alan just sat in the cafeteria with me, right past lunch, right into the afternoon. He sat there with me even after Mr. Findlay told us to get out, to go to class. Even after Findlay gave us both three days detention, Alan just kept his cool because he knew how upset I was. Then he walked over to Findlay, said something to him and Findlay left. Alan just sat back down and stayed with me until I was human again. That's the kind of guy he is.

After school that day, we didn't even go to detention even though we both knew skipping it would mean big trouble. Instead, Alan took me down to Point Pleasant Park and we hiked up to a place he called The Ledge. We sat there on this rock overlooking the Northwest Arm and the ocean. We talked and watched the sun setting. I felt protected and loved. I wasn't just a screwed up kid from a screwed up home. After that I knew I could handle anything anybody wanted to say about me at school.

But that was months ago. Now I counted the minutes until my parents went to bed. Then, I tiptoed down the stairs and went out.

I could have caught a bus, but it would have taken too long to wait—so I walked the four kilometres to the hospital. I walked fast and I ran part of the way. Once a car slowed down beside me, but I didn't even turn to see who it was. I kept my legs moving and didn't look back.

More hassles were ahead of me at the hospital. I tried to calm down, but knew I looked frazzled when I got to the front desk.

"I need to see my brother, Alan Richards," I lied to the nurse. "He had an accident and he's here somewhere."

She checked through some lists. "He's in intensive care. You can't go in."

"But there must be something somebody can tell me," I pleaded.

She could see I was desperate. "There's a waiting room on the third floor. I'll see if I can get one of the night-duty doctors to come by."

"Thanks," I said and ran for the elevator.

When I opened the door to the waiting room, I saw Alan's parents huddled together on a sofa.

"How is he?" I asked them.

Mrs. Richards looked up at me and only had one thing to say: "You have no business here." Then she began to cry.

I stood my ground, trying to figure out what I had ever done to get this lady so down on me. Right now it seemed like the stupidest thing on earth for her to have a grudge against me. How could I get through to her that I cared about Alan too, and that I had a right to be here?

Alan's father patted her on the shoulder and got up. He walked me to the other side of the room and whispered, "We have a lot to deal with right now. You're not family— you shouldn't be here." He was trying to sound cool and unemotional.

"Can't you at least tell me how he is?"

He sighed. "O.K. Here's what we know. It's a very unusual sort of accident. The doctor says he's never seen anything quite like this happening before . . . at least not from a soccer game. There's some sort of damage to . . . one of his organs . . . his liver. It's not functioning properly. They're hooking him up to a machine."

"Machine?" I said. I didn't understand.

"It's no big deal," he said. "Everything is under control."

I didn't believe him. It *was* a big deal. "Is he going to live?"

Mr. Richards grew angry at me. Was it because I had asked the question they had been avoiding? "Everything is going to be all right, Tina," he told me. "This is just . . . one of those things. It's not a life or death situation."

He sounded sure. But I could tell that underneath all his talk, he was as scared as I was.

"Now go on home," he told me. "You're upsetting my wife."

I saw a doctor come out of Intensive Care. I rushed toward him. "Can you tell me how Alan Richards is doing?" I asked him. I wanted to hear the news straight from the doctor, not just from Alan's old man.

He looked at his clipboard, then at me. "Who are you?"

"Tina," I said, "Alan's girlfriend." Why didn't I have a right to know something?

"So you're Tina," he said. "That boy in there wasn't even conscious when he started calling out your name. Then, when he did wake up, he started giving us one heck of a hard time. He started pulling out the tubes. We had to restrain him. He kept saying he wanted to get up and go find you."

"She can't go in," Mrs. Richards butted in.

I was furious, but knew better than to argue.

"Any news?" Alan's father asked the doctor.

"He's stable for now. Unconscious again, I'm afraid, but stable," the doctor said.

"Good," said his father. "Then everything is going to be O.K." He said it like life was going to shift back to normal.

Somehow I knew better. I had this feeling that Alan's father was trying to convince himself and his wife that there was no real danger. But that wasn't what I read in the doctor's eyes.

CHAPTER 4

Six days went by and no one would tell me a thing. When I called Alan's house, his father would just say, "He's fine," and then hang up. I tried getting up to the third floor in the hospital again, but each time someone told me that I wasn't allowed.

Nobody else at school knew anything, but the rumour was that Alan was getting better. He just had to stay in the hospital for "a while." I tried to believe that, but it was still one of the toughest weeks of my life. I flunked every test that came my way. I couldn't even read three lines in a book without forgetting what I had just read.

I was at my locker after fifth period and who showed up but Rick. He was chewing bubble gum and blowing a big pink balloon of it in my face. Rick hugged his motorcycle helmet like he'd been doing all week around school. His parents had bought him a new Kawasaki. Carrying around the helmet was his way of bragging about his new toy in front of everyone. Rick saw me staring at it.

"I'll take you for a ride sometime," he said.

"Forget it," I replied. "I wouldn't trust you even if you had training wheels on the thing."

Rick looked a little hurt, but he didn't take my cue to get lost. He had something else on his mind. "So, are you going to the unveiling of the new, improved Alan Richards today?"

"What are you talking about?"

He sucked the gum back in and it caught on his cheek. He tried to untangle it from the puny growth of hair on his top lip.

"We got invited to visit the fallen hero," he said sarcastically. "You know, the living legend of the soccer field who lasted a full three minutes into the season."

I wanted to slap the smirk off his face, but I had to know more. "Who invited you?"

"His mom."

It figured. Leave it to Alan's mom to invite a dork like Rick to go see Alan and not me.

Still, it sounded like good news—it meant Alan was improving. I heaved a sigh of relief.

"What time?" I asked.

"Three-thirty."

"What room?"

Rick took out a slip of paper and read the number. "Three fifty-seven." Then he popped his gum into the slip of paper, wadded it up and batted it with the palm of his hand across the hallway.

"Should be good for a laugh," he said.

I slammed the locker and walked away. All I could think was that I was going to get to see Alan. I would be there, invited or not.

I got to the waiting room at 3:30, and this time no one stopped me. When I walked off the elevator I heard the snickering first, then I saw Wicket, Rick, Dorfman, and Leach— all guys from the team.

Coach Kenner was there too, looking uncomfortable as he always did off the playing field. He took me aside and spoke in a hushed voice so no one else would hear. "Tina, I was really impressed with the way you reacted on the field. You handled the whole situation well. You got guts, kid."

I should have felt good about that, but I just wanted to get in to see Alan. I didn't care about anything else.

"Hi, Tina," Wicket said, trying to be polite.

"Thought you weren't invited," Rick teased. He knew there was tension between Alan's folks and me. I said nothing.

The door to 357 opened and Alan's father walked out. "Thanks for coming, guys. Come on in. Alan's anxious to see you. Thanks for coming, coach."

I slinked in last and stood near the back of the room, trying to avoid looking at Alan's father. I was relieved that Mrs. Richards wasn't around.

Then I saw Alan, propped up in bed. I almost didn't recognize him. His face looked sort of greenish-white and his eyes were kind of sunken in. He had one tube going up his nose and another going into his arm. Everywhere I looked there was white tape and tubes hooked up to dripping bottles.

Alan was trying to smile, but having a hard time faking it. I was a bit off to the side and Alan didn't realize I was in the room. I wanted to go right over and give him a hug, but I didn't want to make a scene.

"How's it going, dude?" Dorfman asked.

"This stupid hospital sucks," Alan said. "The only way I'm gonna get better is if those turkey doctors give me a little more freedom." He sounded macho, tough, the way he talked when he was around the guys.

Alan hadn't seen me yet. I was still kind of hiding behind the coach. Even if Mr. Richards was going to throw me out, I'd try to hang around as long as I could.

"Did we win?" Alan asked. Everybody knew what he meant.

"Nah," Rick answered. "We lost by one goal. If you'd made your shot it would have been a tie." Good old Rick wanted to rub it in, even now.

"Easy, dude," Dorfman said, putting an elbow in Rick's ribs. Then he turned to Alan. "When you getting out?"

Alan shrugged. His father interjected, "We don't know for sure when he can get out. Internal injuries. His liver has been damaged. He's still bleeding inside."

"Gross," Leach responded.

Then Alan's father changed his tone. "Don't worry. Alan will be back on the field in no time."

"Tough break," Rick said. "Hard to stay in shape when you're in a hospital bed." He flexed his muscles like he was trying to get the most out of it. Dorfman smacked him on the side of the head.

"How's school?" Alan asked, sounding half asleep. Maybe it was the drugs. He could have been on painkillers.

It was kind of weird that the coach was the one to answer. He hadn't opened his mouth yet. "School is going just great. It looks like we're going to be able to get the new sod for the field."

I could tell that Alan wasn't impressed.

After that it seemed that nobody knew what to say. They shuffled their feet, stared down at the floor. The room grew quiet, too quiet. There was only the sound of liquid dripping down a tube and emptying into an attached plastic bag. Rick nodded toward it to draw everyone's attention. Alan seemed not to notice. I think he was fading off to sleep or something.

I saw the tube coming out from under the sheet. It was clear and the fluid inside was a sickly yellow with streaks of red.

"I think I'm going to be sick," Leach said, and looked around the room for a place to puke. All he found was a trash can. He threw himself over it and heaved out his lunch.

The coach got mad. "Would you pull yourselves together!" he said.

But Wicket and Dorfman looked like they were about to heave as well, only they held their noses and ran for the door. The coach led Leach out of the room, his head hung in embarrassment. Rick and I stood there. Rick had a stupid grin on his face like he thought it was all happening for his personal entertainment. I shoved him toward the door and he took the hint. Mr. Richards carried the trash can out, closing the door quietly behind him.

I'm not sure if Alan knew what had freaked out the guys. And I don't know if he knew that I wasn't supposed to be there. But he saw me then for the first time.

I walked up beside him and he held up his hand. I grabbed onto it and gave a squeeze. Alan squeezed back, but didn't seem to have much strength. I leaned over and put my cheek up to his. I closed my eyes and didn't realize he was crying until I felt his tears on my cheek. "God, Tina, it's good to see you," he whispered. "I didn't think you were ever coming."

"I've been trying. I wanted to see you so much," I said. I wanted to explain why, but I didn't want to upset him. I left it at that.

"Stay with me," Alan said. He held me close to him. "Tina, you have to get me out of here. I just can't stand being stuck in this prison any longer."

I didn't know what to say. I held him tight and said, "It's going to be O.K." I tried to sound convincing, but I knew it was a lie. A lie I wanted both of us to believe.

CHAPTER 5

After that, nobody tried to stop me from visiting Alan. Of course, I didn't feel comfortable hanging around when Alan's parents were there. Every day, Alan's father would say something to him like, "You look a lot better today, kid. You're coming along great."

But around his parents and doctors, Alan was pretty snippy. "If I'm doing so great, then why don't you let me out of here. Man, I need to breathe some real air, you know," he told his father. He'd been in the hospital for ten days.

Later, when everyone else was out of the room, Alan acted differently. He wanted me to sit up close beside him on the bed and asked me how I was doing in school. "Any of the guys hassling you or anything?"

I told him that I was doing O.K. "I just miss having you around, that's all."

I held out my hand to him. "Squeeze my hand," I said. "Hard." It was my little test to try to figure out if he really was getting better.

He squeezed and I could tell he was putting all his strength into it. But he certainly wasn't as strong as he used to be.

"I don't care what it takes," he told me. "I'm getting out of here. I just can't stand being cooped up and treated like somebody's biology experiment. The longer I stay here, the more I think I'll never get out. If I just had a chance to get outside, to go home, or go anywhere, I'd get better. I know it."

The door opened and two doctors came in. I recognized Dr. Bennington, the young doctor who had been there from the start. He'd been a regular, but the other guy was new.

While they were in the room, Alan seemed even more frustrated. When the door closed behind them, he whispered to me, "I wish I knew what was going on. Nobody tells me anything."

I had to look away just then because I couldn't quite handle seeing Alan look so helpless. I ruffled his hair and got up.

"I'll be right back," I said. I decided to try to talk to Dr. Bennington myself. Maybe Alan's parents knew the whole truth. But I knew Alan didn't and I sure didn't know all the facts.

I saw Bennington and the other doctor standing in the hallway talking. I walked past them and stationed myself just inside the door of the waiting room. I sat down on the floor and kept the door open with my foot so I could hear what they were saying.

"I estimate that the liver is only working at about ten per cent," Bennington said. "The machine and the drugs aren't enough."

The other doctor agreed and added, "He needs continual transfusions. But our supplies of B positive blood are running low."

"I don't think we have much choice," the other doctor said. "He needs the transplant."

I felt a cold wave of panic come over me. I didn't really understand what they were saying, but it sounded scary.

"But look at the blood type," Dr. Bennington said. "Do you realize how hard it will be to find a matching organ donor?"

"Yes, but without a transplant, he could die. Even if he stays hooked up to everything and even if we keep him stocked in fresh blood, the odds are still bad for him."

That's when a nurse opened the door and just about tripped over me. I jumped up and said I was sorry. Bennington saw me and realized I had overheard their discussion.

"What were you doing there?" the nurse demanded.

I ignored her.

"What is it you need to save Alan?" I asked Dr. Bennington. I wasn't sure I understood what they had been talking about . . . something about a transplant, but I didn't understand the rest.

Dr. Bennington took off his glasses.

"Is Alan going to die?" I demanded. I had to know.

"We're doing everything we can," he said. "Today I'll put out a call to hospitals for a possible donor."

"What about me?" I asked, not knowing what I was saying. "Could I be a donor?"

Dr. Bennington shook his head. "You only have one liver. And you can't live without it. The donor has to be already dead. The blood has to match and . . . we have to have permission to use the liver."

I felt like everything was collapsing around me.

"But we do need blood," the other doctor said, seeing my despair. "What's your blood type?"

I shrugged. I didn't know.

He pulled a note pad out of his pocket, scratched something down, and handed it to me. "Two flights down. They'll only take a little to see if you're the right type."

I took the paper and headed toward the elevator, my head dizzy. I was praying that I had the right blood type. I'd give as much as I could if it would help keep Alan alive. Then I stopped, realizing that Alan would be wondering where I'd gone.

"Don't worry," Dr. Bennington called after me. "I'll tell your boyfriend you'll be back."

CHAPTER 6

I was sitting in another waiting room, this time praying that the test would come out right. I was hoping that I would have the right match—B positive, whatever that meant.

I spent twenty minutes looking at *People* magazine, until the nurse returned with a form. "Take this back to Dr. Bennington," she said, sealing it in an envelope.

On the way up the elevator, I looked inside the envelope. I couldn't wait. I didn't really understand most of it, but there it was—Blood type: A negative. So I wouldn't even be able to donate my blood to help Alan. When I found Dr. Bennington and handed him the envelope, he could tell by the look on my face that I wasn't going to be a blood donor.

"It was a long shot," he said. "B positive or B negative is O.K., but nothing else will work."

Well, maybe *I* couldn't give Alan exactly what he needed, but at least I could make sure he had enough of a blood supply. I started asking everyone I knew what type blood they had and if they'd donate blood to the hospital.

"Hey, if Alan can use my blood, he can have all he wants," Dorfman said.

"Same here," Wicket added. "And I'll talk to the coach. Every guy on the team should go get a blood test to find out."

That cheered me up a little. "Thanks," I said. I felt a bit better toward these guys, even though they'd made such a mess of things at the hospital the other day.

After a few days I saw Coach Kenner in the hall. "Tina, I collected the results from the team and there's only one type B. It's Rick," he said. "Go figure that."

I was a little shocked, but it didn't matter. Rick's blood was as good as anyone's.

I scouted the school for the rest of the day looking for Rick, but he was nowhere to be found. Wicket hinted that Rick had cut a few classes and was cruising around on his bike.

But he'd be back before school was over. "He hates to miss a chance to have everybody gawking at him on his new toy," Wicket told me with a big grin on his face.

It wasn't until the end of school, just as I was closing up my locker, that Rick showed up. I could smell his breath and knew that he'd been drinking.

"I hear you've been looking for me," he said. "What do you want?" He had his stupid motorcycle helmet under one arm and a big grin on his face.

"You had your blood tested, right?"

"Yeah, so?" Rick said in a real smug voice.

I couldn't believe that I used to think he was a great guy. We'd had some really good times together. But ever since I broke up with him, it was like he was looking for some way to get back at me . . . or to get back at Alan. The guy just seemed like a jerk. And now he was a jerk with a motorcycle, which was twice as bad. He set his helmet down on the floor between us, and when he straightened up he wobbled a little.

"So what was it?" I asked him.

"B something or other. I don't know."

"You're the only one so far with the right blood type. Can you go down and donate some blood at the hospital . . . for Alan?"

Suddenly Rick seemed to stop being such a tough guy. Maybe it was the booze, or maybe he was really worried about Alan, too. "Sure," he said. "I'll donate as much as they can pump out of me. Then will you believe I'm not such a rotten guy?"

This sudden change in Rick threw me off. I tried to make eye contact with him, but he looked away from me and back toward the door. For a split second, I recognized what I had seen in Rick. Underneath the tough macho shell, he was hurt and lonely.

I was trying hard to think of the right thing to say, but I couldn't find the words.

"Rick . . . " I began, but he shook his head and started to drift away from me.

"Ah, forget I said that. Don't worry, I'll donate the blood. Pretty soon, ole Al will be back on the scene and I'll be just a faded memory."

"Wait," I said. I didn't want him walking away like this. And he seemed very unsteady on his feet.

I had a hard time squeezing the rest of my books into my locker. When I closed it and started after Rick, I saw that his helmet was sitting on the floor. I grabbed it and ran down the hallway. When I got outside, Rick had already taken off on his motorcycle and was speeding down Robie Street.

I threw his helmet down on the ground in frustration. Rick's driver's licence fell out from where it had been tucked inside. I picked it up and stared at it, then stuck it in my back pocket. Looking off in the direction where Rick had gone, I said, "I'm sorry." But there was no one around to hear my apology.

CHAPTER 7

I decided against going to see Alan after school. I didn't want to take the chance of running into Alan's mother at the hospital. Things got a bit ugly if we were there at the same time. First she'd say something nasty to me, then Alan would start yelling at her to back off. Next thing you knew, she'd start crying and Alan would get really upset. Maybe if I stayed away for a couple of days, things would mellow out.

My house was empty as usual. I tried to watch TV, but couldn't concentrate.

Boy, I was angry at the way things were going. Dr. Bennington made it sound like it was unlikely they would find a liver for Alan. "We're doing as much as we can," he had said. "Unless we find a donor, there's not much else we can do except keep the machine running and hope." The big trouble was that the donor had to be dead first.

I felt like people weren't doing enough to help. And I was feeling frustrated that I couldn't do more. I must have dozed off into a fitful sleep there on the sofa.

Then the doorbell rang. I shook the sleep out of me and went to the door. I was amazed to see Alan's mother and father standing outside.

"Who do you think you are, spreading rumours about Alan's condition around school?" Alan's mother snapped at me as soon as I opened the door. "We've told you to stop interfering." Behind her was Mr. Richards, looking quite uncomfortable.

"I've only been trying to help," I said.

"You haven't been helping," she snapped back. "Every time you visit, Alan gets more upset."

"We've come to see your parents," Mr. Richards interjected, with a shade more cool in his voice.

"They're not here," I said. "And you're wrong. Alan wants me to visit him."

"You're interfering. We've already asked you to keep out of it," Alan's father said, trying to sound reasonable. "We've got doctors there, some of the best trained men in the country." He said the word "men" like that was what counted. Men could handle these things. Not women. And especially not girls.

"But Alan could die!" I told them.

"It's not true!" Mrs. Richards cried out. She started to cry.

Mr. Richards looked at me and his voice dropped. "Who told you that?"

"I overheard Dr. Bennington talking to another doctor. Alan doesn't just need more blood. He needs a transplant, too."

"Is it true?" Mrs. Richards looked at her husband. Suddenly it dawned on me that she hadn't been told.

Mr. Richards nodded his head without speaking. Mrs. Richards seemed stunned.

"I don't know what we're going to do," Alan's father said, choking back tears.

Then the phone rang. It rang twice before I could move to answer it. The call was from the hospital.

"Tina? It's Dr. Bennington. Do you know where Alan is? Is he with you?"

"I don't understand. No, of course he's not here," I said.

"He's not in his room. He's just . . . well, he's disappeared," Dr. Bennington explained. The nurses say he was acting a little funny. Then he started asking for you again. He wanted to know why you weren't there and then said he had to go meet you somewhere. I talked to him for a bit and he seemed to settle down, but then, later, the nurse told me he wasn't in bed. He must have changed into his street clothes when no one was around and just left. It's quite possible he was delirious. I tried his parents' house, but there was no answer. Then we thought of you. We had your name and address from the blood clinic. We thought you might have some idea where he's gone."

"What will happen to him without . . . without all the tubes and stuff?" I didn't have the right words, but I knew he was in serious trouble.

"I don't know. He might pass out, go into shock."

"Could he die?" I asked, my voice trembling.

Alan's father grabbed the phone from me. "What's happened to our son?" he demanded.

Fear crept over Mrs. Richards' face.

"We'll check everywhere," Alan's father told Bennington, and then hung up the phone.

"What happened?" Mrs. Richards asked.

"He's missing from the hospital," her husband said. "He'd been acting funny and said something about going to meet Tina."

Mrs. Richards glared at me accusingly.

I shook my head. "I didn't know about it."

"Let's get over to the hospital and check the neighbourhood," Mr. Richards said to his wife. "He can't be too far away."

Mrs. Richards said nothing. She didn't have to. Her expression said it for her: *It's all your fault, Tina.*

Right then I didn't care what she thought. I knew Alan was in real danger. "I'm coming too," I insisted.

CHAPTER 8

Alan's mother couldn't stop me. But all the way to the hospital she lectured me about what a bad influence I'd been on her son.

"Alan and I are good for each other," I insisted. I couldn't see why she wanted to trash me at a time like this. She should have been worrying about how we were going to find Alan.

"He'd never even had a detention before he met you," she went on. "That's the kind of influence you've had on him."

Mr. Richards was driving like a maniac. He'd just gone through a red light and come within inches of picking off two women waiting at a corner. He swerved to avoid them, then squealed the tires as he raced on toward the hospital.

"Alan was never like this before!" she went on.

I could see that Alan's father was as fed up with her complaining as I was. I should have kept my mouth shut, but I couldn't.

"All I ever did was suggest that he'd be better off if he thought for himself. Maybe he should stop accepting your rules all the time." There, I'd said it.

She turned around from the front seat and gave me an icy stare. "And if he weren't always trying to think for himself, he might still be in the hospital bed—not out in the street somewhere."

Mr. Richards slowed down to make the turn into the hospital parking lot. I'd taken all I could stand. I threw open the door and jumped out just as he pulled to a stop. Now was not the time for arguing. Now was the time for finding Alan.

Every minute counted. I decided to go around to the back of the building and start there. Where would Alan go? I jogged down South Street, hoping for a miracle I guess, hoping that I'd see him just walking along. Alan had always been tough. Before the accident, I'd seen him keep playing in a game even after he'd had the wind knocked out of him. Once he set his mind to something, he usually found a way of doing it.

I came to the corner of Tower Road. I didn't have any idea which way to go. The hopelessness of everything was starting to get to me. Across the street was a cemetery. An awful feeling swept over me. Alan could be anywhere. He could be dying. How was I going to find him in time? Which way should I go?

Then something clicked. I knew which way to go, but I didn't quite know why. I began to run. It was like my legs already knew the way. I asked myself, *Why south? Why this way?* I was afraid to stop. I was headed down Tower Road. Why would he go this way?

And then something told me what my legs already knew. Point Pleasant Park was this way. It was the part of the city closest to the ocean. Alan always loved the sea. After he had first taken me there the day I was so upset, we had gone back on our bicycles dozens of times.

I ran harder until my lungs ached. It seemed impossible that Alan could have made it all the way to the park, but I didn't know where else to try. This had to be it.

When I ran through the big iron gates into the parking lot, I saw a taxi parked by the hiking trail.

Maybe, just maybe.

I banged hard on the window. The driver was eating a sandwich and listening to a ball game on the radio. He looked annoyed as he rolled down the window.

"I'm looking for somebody," I said. I described Alan as best as I could. I was so out of breath that my words came out in short bursts.

"Take it easy," the guy said. "I gave that kid a lift down here not much more than twenty minutes ago. Picked him up by the hospital."

"Was he O.K.?"

"He didn't look that great, to tell you the truth. He on drugs or something?"

"No," I said. "But he's sick. Which way did he go?"

He pointed down the forest path.

If I had been using my brain I would have phoned the hospital right then or asked somebody for help. Instead, I took off and ran down the wide forest path. I passed a cop on a horse and a bunch of kids my own age who were throwing pine cones at each other. Seeing them made me feel the difference. They were kids, still goofing off. For me, everything was different. And if I was wrong with my guess, maybe the whole world was about to collapse for me.

I headed west on a narrow trail. Up ahead was the rock outcropping that looked out over the Northwest Arm of the harbour and on out to sea. It was our place. I started up the final bit of steep trail leading to The Ledge. I had begun to climb up when I saw him. Alan! I touched his hand even before I could see his face. His hand felt cold.

He looked like he was curled up asleep. I bent over him and put my ear to his mouth. My heart was racing so fast and I was breathing so hard that at first I couldn't tell. Then I held my breath and waited. I felt his

breath on my cheek. He was alive—but he wasn't O.K.

I knew the problem wasn't on the outside. It wasn't anything you could see. His breath was shallow and jerky. I had to get him back to the hospital fast, but I couldn't carry him down. I wasn't strong enough and besides, I might hurt him more.

I think the hardest thing in the world for me to do just then was to leave him. All I had on was a light jacket and I threw it over him. Then I scrambled down from The Ledge and ran for the cop on the horse.

When I got to the main pathway I stopped two guys on mountain bikes. I asked one to phone an ambulance, the other to go south in search of the cop I'd seen. They could tell from how freaked-out I was that I was serious. Both sped off in opposite directions. All I could do was wait for help to come— and pray that it would come fast enough to save Alan's life.

CHAPTER 9

The ambulance attendant, Martha, recognized me almost at once.

"You're getting to be a regular customer," she said as we got into the ambulance.

I was shaking—just plain scared. She cupped an oxygen mask over Alan and put a blanket around me. I was really glad it was her. She seemed to have everything under control.

"It wasn't my idea," I said. "He should have stayed in the hospital."

She gave me a curious glance. "Nobody said it was, honey. You've got to relax. Boy, you sure have your hands full looking after this guy. You sure he's worth all the trouble?"

"Yeah, he's worth it," I said. I liked her. I knew that she was teasing me in a gentle way and trying to make things seem less scary than they really were. I knew she was someone I could trust. While we talked, the driver was whipping down the street with his siren going.

"Shut that damn thing off," Martha said. "We're almost there. So just can it."

The siren wound down with a mournful howl fading off to nothing.

"Know anything about how a liver works?" I asked her.

She shrugged. "Can't live without it. That his problem?"

"Yeah, I guess he needs a new one or he dies."

"Transplant time?"

"If they find a donor in time."

We backed into the ambulance loading bay and had just come to a stop when another ambulance came roaring in beside us. That driver had the siren up full blast. It was murder on the ears. Two hospital guys in white were about to unload Alan when the driver of the other ambulance yelled, "This one first. Got to get him in quick!"

The two hospital orderlies turned and

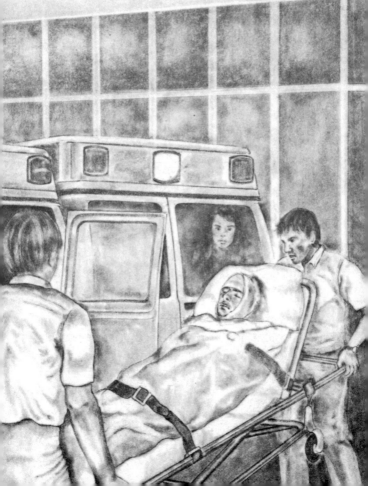
Emergency

went to the other ambulance.

I jumped out and started after them. "Wait!"

But Martha grabbed hold of my shoulders. "Just be calm. Your boyfriend's more or less stable. That, over there, sounds very bad."

I heard the driver say, "Motorcycle accident. The kid went into a car. Head injury. Looks bad."

As the cart came past us, a doctor was already sidling up to get a look. When he pulled back the bandage, I got an awful look at the victim. I almost didn't recognize him at first, but then I knew who it was. I watched as they wheeled Rick through the open doors and out of view.

Two other attendants came out and unloaded Alan. I walked with them as far as the door and then Martha tugged me back again. "Come on," she said. "I'll buy you a coffee." I guess she had seen my face as they wheeled Rick past. She didn't know what the story was, but she knew I needed a friend. Right then I felt like the world had gone hopelessly insane.

In the hospital cafeteria, I explained everything to Martha. She listened. I didn't touch the coffee. "Rick is a jerk, but now I feel like his accident was somehow my fault."

"It wasn't your fault. He didn't like to wear his helmet. You said so yourself."

"But he didn't deserve this."

"Honey, most people who get hurt don't deserve it."

"Now Rick's the one who's going to need blood. And there's not a thing I can do to help either one of them."

Martha gave me a soft, sad look. "I'm afraid you just have to trust the system."

I knew she was trying to be helpful, but right then I didn't trust anybody or anything. Martha was off duty now and she stayed with me for at least two hours there in the cafeteria. Every twenty minutes she went to check to see if there was any news. I felt like screaming, but somehow she kept me calmed down.

Then Dr. Bennington walked into the cafeteria and came over to us. "Alan's conscious," he told me. "You can go see him."

Alan was propped up in bed. This time he didn't have a tube shoved up his nose. It was good to see him smile. I sat down on the edge of the bed, almost afraid to touch him, afraid I might injure him in some way.

"I knew you'd know where I'd be," he said.

"Yeah. That's our place."

"Except it wasn't supposed to be like that. I'm sorry."

I shrugged. "Have they told you everything?" I asked.

"I hope so. All they say is that I stay hooked up to the machine until a better option comes along."

"A transplant?" I wanted to be sure he knew.

"Yeah, a transplant. Like in the Frankenstein movies." He was looking pretty tired again.

"I always kind of liked the Frankenstein monster," I told him. "He was my hero for a while. A very misunderstood character."

Alan tried a brave smile. His energy was fading and I knew he was very tired. "Tina, when I woke up here and they told me you tracked me down, I got to thinking. I can't believe I've put you through all this. I think you'd better leave me alone for a while and see what happens."

"Oh sure," I said. I was angry he was even saying this. This was just like Alan. Trying to tough things out on his own.

"No kidding. I'm not much fun like, well, like this." He pointed down to the wires and tubes going under the sheets. "It's been rough on you. So just forget about me until it's all over one way or the other."

I took a deep breath. "Right," I said with a smirk on my face. "Give up on a chance to hang out with the Frankenstein monster? No way." I kissed him on the cheek.

Maybe I should have kept quiet, but I thought Alan should know. "Rick got himself messed up on his new motorcycle," I told him. "He's downstairs."

Alan leaned forward. "How is he?"

"I don't know," I admitted.

"There goes the season," Alan said. What a weird thing—he was still thinking about soccer after all this. But then I realized he hadn't seen what I had.

"Coach will be really ticked off," I said, playing along with him, when suddenly I saw something happen. It was like the blood just drained out of his face. He lifted his arm and reached out to touch me. I grabbed onto his hand and felt how cold and clammy it was. At first I thought he was just falling asleep, but then one of the machines started to beep. I turned toward the door to call for help. Two nurses and an orderly came running down the hall.

I tried to keep holding onto Alan's hand, but they pushed me back out of the way.

Dr. Bennington came in and checked Alan's chest with a stethoscope, then stared at the monitor. "Heart's O.K.," he said, "but we need another transfusion. He must have bruised the liver again."

One of the nurses ran off as the other prepared Alan for another IV. Bennington pulled an oxygen mask down over Alan's face and was checking his pulse. He looked up at me. "You'll have to leave the room."

Alan's parents were there in the hall. "What's going on?" Mr. Richards demanded.

"Dr. Bennington has it under control," one of the nurses said.

Mrs. Richards grabbed my sleeve. "You had it all planned, didn't you?"

"What are you talking about?" I asked.

"You could have killed him—getting him to meet you at the park," she said.

"It wasn't my idea!" I snapped. I didn't need to take any of her garbage.

Mr. Richards stood behind me. "I've talked with the administration. This time, they assure me, you won't be allowed in Alan's room. And you're not to keep bothering Dr. Bennington. You're getting in the way."

I spun around, outraged. How could they have it so wrong?

CHAPTER 10

Disgusted, I walked toward the front door. I felt like a criminal.

Martha was sitting in the front lobby by the glass doors. "What's up?" she asked.

"Alan's pretty bad off," I said, "and his parents think it's all my fault. I'm not even allowed to see him any more." I started crying. Martha put her arm around me. "Any news about Rick?" I asked her.

Martha shook her head.

I couldn't help but remember what Rick looked like on the stretcher. He looked so awful I wished I hadn't seen him. "I feel really rotten about everything. Like a vampire or something."

"I don't get it."

"Alan's got B positive blood," I said, trying to explain. "And guess who else does?"

"Rick?"

"Yeah," I answered. My mind kept going back to the last time Rick and I talked in the hallway. I could still see his motorcycle helmet sitting on the floor. I pulled out his driver's licence that I had put in my pocket after it had fallen out. I read his name, his address, the date he was born. The image of Rick's face, all bloody, came into my head. And then something else. What I was thinking just then was scary. And awful. And I was feeling so ashamed.

Martha said it out loud for me. "And if Rick dies, you've got yourself an organ donor."

I couldn't look at her just then. A flood of tears came out of me.

"Tina, whether Rick lives or dies has nothing to do with you. And whatever you think right now will make no difference to Rick's chances."

"I guess I know that. And I don't really want him to die. It's just that . . . if he does die, it's a chance for Alan to live. Especially now. I think he's quite a bit worse off after running away from the hospital."

"I'm gonna see what I can find out about Rick," Martha said. "I'll be back as soon as I can."

The minutes stretched out as I waited. Martha came back as promised. "How is he?" I asked.

"Nobody wants to say for sure," Martha said. "They really don't like to make predictions in these kinds of cases."

"But what does that mean? Is he going to be O.K.?"

Martha looked down at the floor. "It was a very severe head injury," she said. "He's on life support, the sort they use for patients who are what they call 'brain dead.' If the parents agree, they might shut the support down. If there's nothing more they can do . . ."

I started to cry. Already, I missed Rick. I missed his obnoxious, macho jokes and his stupid jealousy. I missed that stuck-up way he walked around school.

Outside, a car skidded to a stop. Then I saw something that made me suck in my breath and cover my face with my hands. Rick's mother and father came through the door and ran past us. I'll never forget the looks on their faces.

Martha understood what was happening. She put her arm around me and began walking me outside. "Go home," she said. "I'll tell Dr. Bennington what you told me about Rick's blood type. If it looks like Rick isn't going to pull through, he'll talk to Rick's parents. That's all we can do." She gave me a gentle push.

I didn't go home right away, but walked back to The Ledge, climbed up and watched the sun setting. It had a sad, beautiful quality that made me think about Rick and Alan and how stupid life was. Then I walked home in the dark and had a lousy night's sleep. Every time I woke up, I kept hoping it was all a bad dream and would go away. But it didn't.

I couldn't go to school the next morning. Instead, I went back to the hospital. I got as far as the waiting room in the Outpatient Clinic before someone came up from behind me and grabbed my arm.

"This way." It was Martha.

"What are you still doing here?" I asked.

"You need a friend, Tina. I'm all you've got. And it looks like Alan's folks are serious about keeping you away from Alan and Dr. Bennington as well. By the way, you look like hell."

"Thanks," I said. I let her lead me outside.

"Get in," she said when we got to her ambulance.

"Why?"

"Just do it."

I got in and she told me to lie down on the gurney. I lay down and covered myself with a sheet. Martha opened the back door and wheeled me out onto the ramp and back inside the hospital.

"I'm not supposed to be doing stuff like this," she told me. She sounded nervous.

We travelled up in a crowded elevator and I pretended to be unconscious. When she wheeled me off on the fourth floor, she had to lie to the women at the nursing station to get by.

"He's in his office," Martha said, looking through the glass door. "Don't knock. Just go in."

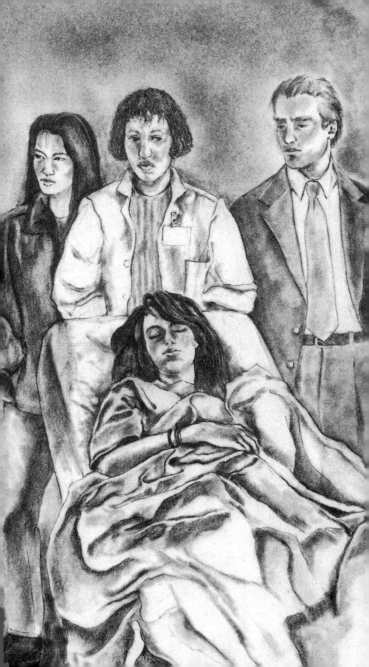

I pulled off the sheet, jumped up and went in through the door, closing it hard behind me.

Dr. Bennington was startled. He looked up from a pile of papers on his desk. "I don't believe you have an appointment," he said, more annoyed than angry.

"Did you talk to Rick Evans' parents?" I blurted out.

Dr. Bennington seemed surprised. "I talked to them about a half hour ago." I waited for him to say more, but he sat silently with his fingers locked together in front of him.

"Is Rick alive?"

At first I thought Dr. Bennington wasn't going to answer. Then he said it. "He can't recover. There was major damage to the brain."

I closed my eyes.

"Rick told me his blood was type B," I said.

"He wasn't lying. It's a perfect match."

Dr. Bennington knew what I wanted to know next, knew it would be hard for me to ask. I didn't have to.

"They refused," he said softly.

"But they can't do that!" I said. "If Rick is going to die and Alan stands a chance to live, then he deserves that chance."

He sighed. "It's their right. They're suffering a terrible loss. That's hard for them."

"Can I talk to them?"

Suddenly he turned cold and professional. "Absolutely not," he said. "Tina, we've got calls in to over thirty donor hospitals. Something will come up."

"Right," I said. I didn't believe a word of it. Finding a donor with B type blood was going to be nearly impossible. Nothing had come up so far. The odds were stacked against it.

"We're doing all we can."

"It's not enough," I said, my voice trembling.

CHAPTER 11

I took the stairs down to the third floor. As I passed Alan's room I looked in. Both of his parents were there. His mother was crying and his father was pacing back and forth. Alan was unconscious. As I pushed up against the glass of the door to get a better look, I could see his skin was an awful colour. I knew that was because his liver wasn't working. He was getting worse and time was running out.

I felt frozen, totally helpless. I didn't think I could move away from that spot. But someone was walking at a fast clip toward me. I didn't turn around to look. It was Martha again. She gave me a pat on the shoulder.

We walked toward the elevator and got on. As we began to go down, she punched the red "Stop" button and we came to a halt between floors.

"What did Rick's parents say?"

"They said no."

Martha cursed under her breath.

"I have to talk to them," I told her. "I have to convince them." Even as I said it, I didn't know if I had the courage. I was scared to death that I wouldn't say the right thing, that I would mess it up somehow and it would be all over. "But I don't know if I can do it," I said.

Martha took my hand and squeezed it. She looked me straight in the eye. Then she punched the button again with her other hand. The elevator started moving again and she pushed the button for the second floor.

The doors parted. She held them open and pointed down the hall. "Third door down. Wait until there's no doctor or nurse inside."

I guess I knew then that there was nothing in the world that could have stopped me from trying. I walked down the hall and knocked gently on the door frame. Then I went in.

Rick's head was almost completely bandaged. There were machines beeping and ticking. I think Rick's parents were praying. They looked up when I came in.

I had met Rick's parents only twice before, back when Rick and I were going together. They were pretty old-fashioned, but they spoiled Rick by giving him anything he wanted. That's why he had the motorcycle.

"I'm here to talk about Alan Richards," I said. I kept looking straight at Rick, not at them. I was pretty sure they knew about Alan and me now.

"How dare you!" Rick's dad said, his voice a harsh whisper.

I pretended I didn't hear. I looked at Rick's mother and spoke, hoping the words would do some sort of magic all on their own.

"Rick is probably going to die and it's not going to mean much," I began. "A stupid accident." As I began to give what I figured to be the most important speech of my life, I didn't know what to do with my hands, so I stuck them in my back pockets.

"Get out of here!" Rick's father demanded. I tried to ignore him.

"It's not fair," I went on, "that Rick has to die. I'll miss him very much, although I know it's nothing like what you will feel."

Rick's father started for the door. He was going to have me thrown out. I almost panicked and started crying, but Rick's mother stopped him. "Let's hear what she has to say," she said in a voice full of sadness.

"Rick and Alan were friends," I said. "Well, sort of friends."

"They still are friends," Rick's father insisted.

I could see right then that he wasn't ready to admit his son was dying.

"We know that Rick probably isn't going to make it," Mrs. Evans said, "but we're still hoping for a miracle."

Rick's father just shook his head. He looked angry—like he wanted to hit somebody. He scared me, but I wasn't ready to back off.

"And if Rick dies," I told her, "he can save Alan's life. If you give permission for the transplant."

"We already told the doctors no," Mr. Evans insisted.

"It's against everything we believe," Rick's mom explained softly.

"And it's too much . . . too much to ask at a time like this!" Mr. Evans' hands were clenched into fists. I'm almost sure he was ready to hit me, or to hit something, because he was so angry that he couldn't do anything about his son dying.

I held my ground. "It *is* too much to ask," I told him. "And I'm not supposed to be here asking it. But I'm asking anyway. If Rick dies, his death can be worth something—because he'll be saving another life."

Rick's father was shaking his head. Mrs. Evans was sobbing, but I could see she was trying to get control of herself. I was shaking too, I was so scared. I pulled my hands out of my back pockets and I was holding onto something. I was looking down at Rick's driver's licence.

"Get out!" Mr. Evans said.

"I'm sorry to do this, but I have to," I answered. "I think I know how you feel. And maybe you've never thought about donating part of your son's body if he dies.

But you have to think about it now. Rick was a tough guy and he didn't back down from much. I think he'd be mad at you if you let him back down from this."

I was almost shocked that I had come out and said that. I was sure it was the wrong thing to say. But suddenly Rick's mother looked up at me. "You really did know Rick, didn't you?"

I nodded.

"He just pretended he was tough," his mother said. "Underneath, he was just a little boy trying to act tough."

"I think I knew that."

"He wanted to be the best at everything he did," his father said. "And he sometimes made fun of other kids who didn't try as hard as he did."

I nodded. It was true.

Rick's father didn't seem so angry now. "I think he always wanted to be some kind of hero," he said.

I was staring down at Rick's driver's licence, unfolding it. I kept trying to come up with just the right thing to say, the perfect

words that would make all the difference. I silently read his full name, his birth date, the long serial number. Then I turned over the licence, saw the organ donor statement on the back. Rick had signed his name to it.

I swallowed hard, handed Rick's father the licence. He looked closely at the back, where Rick had signed. "I think Rick finally has his chance," I said softly.

The door opened and three doctors walked in. One of them was Dr. Bennington. He looked angry when he saw me. "I'm sorry," he said to Rick's parents. "This was not supposed to happen."

I looked at Mr. and Mrs. Evans, but they said nothing. They were looking at their son.

I turned to leave. It had all been in vain.

"Wait," Mr. Evans said. I turned around, but he wasn't talking to me. "Dr. Bennington, we need to talk," he said. "And I want Tina to stay to hear what we have to say."

CHAPTER 12

I went by myself to Rick's funeral. I didn't cry even though I was surrounded by all kinds of people in tears. Even Leach and Dorfman and some of the other kids from school were crying.

Rick's mom spotted me after the service. She gripped hard onto my hand and wouldn't let go as all the other adults kept coming up to say how sorry they were. I felt funny, but I just stood there until she was ready to let go. She never said one word to me.

Later, I went to see Alan at the hospital. This time, nobody tried to keep me out of the room. Alan was propped up in bed and he still didn't look too good. "You all right?" I asked.

"Do I look all right?" he snapped.

"You look alive," I said. "That's a start." But I felt hurt. "Are you angry at me?" I asked, sitting down on the bed.

He looked away, clenching his fists. "I'm sorry," he said. "I guess I'm just having a hard time, is all. I keep having these images of Rick smashing up his bike. And I keep thinking about what a jerk the guy was sometimes. And now part of him is inside me and I keep thinking how he saved my life."

I put my arms around him and held him close. "It's confusing," I said. "I know."

Alan nodded, trying to hold back the tears. "And what if it's never the same any more? Are you still going to like me?"

"Don't be silly. Of course I'll like you." Leave it to Alan to use the word "like" at a time like this. It made me feel that he was getting back to normal. "Besides, I don't care if you're different. I think we'll all be different after this."

Just then Alan's parents appeared at the door. They stopped when they saw me. "We'll come back later," Mr. Evans said.

"No," Alan said. "I want you all here."

Alan's parents came in and stood on the other side of the bed from me. "How are you

Tina?" his father said, in a very stiff, formal voice.

"I'm O.K.," I said. I still found it hard to look at Alan's parents. They had made me feel like such a rotten person and it still hurt, even after everything we'd been through.

"Mom?" Alan looked at his mother, waiting for her to do something. His look was angry—but it had all of his old strength in it.

Mrs. Richards looked up at me. She no longer seemed full of the pain and anger. She just seemed embarrassed. "Tina, I'm sorry for the way we treated you. And I'm sorry for all the things I said. I was wrong."

"No apology necessary," I said, but I was lying. I did need to hear her say that. And now I knew for sure that everything was going to be all right.

"You've been a good friend to Alan, the best," Mr. Richards added.

I looked at Alan when I heard the word "friend." We were both thinking the same thing. We were a lot more than friends. But neither one of us said a word.

"I think we should just leave you two alone," Mrs. Richards said. She led her husband out of the room and closed the door.

At first we didn't quite know what to say to each other.

"How do we explain what Rick did for me to all the other guys?" Alan asked.

"We tell them the truth and we make sure they know he was one heck of a guy—that he really was a hero."

I was afraid that maybe Alan was going to get depressed again thinking about Rick. I knew that the time for feeling sorry was just about done.

"Move over," I said, and sat down beside Alan on the hospital bed.

It had been a long time since we had kissed, but as soon as our lips met, I knew that nothing between us had changed. I still felt the same way about him.

"What's it feel like to kiss the Frankenstein monster?" Alan asked.

"Not scary at all," I answered.